The Old Witch's Party

by Ida DeLage

illustrated by Mimi Korach

GARRARD PUBLISHING COMPANY
CHAMPAIGN, ILLINOIS

THE OLD WITCH'S PARTY

It was Halloween.

The old witch was in her cave.

Her fire was dancing.

Her pot of brew was bubbling.

The old witch tasted her brew.

"Hmm," she said.

"Something is not right.

My brew doesn't taste good.

I think it needs

some poison ivy."

The old witch
hopped on her broom.
"I will go and get
some poison ivy," she said.
"My brew has to be very magic."

The old witch flew
to the old oak tree.
Poison ivy was creeping
all around and around.
"Oh, how lovely!" she said.
"Now my brew will be
very magic."

On the way back to her cave,
the old witch looked down.
"Ho!" she said.
"There is the school.
I think I'll peek in."

9

The children were having
a Halloween party!
"I will light
the jack-o'-lantern,"
said the teacher.
"I hope it's not too scary."

10

"Now we will play
Pin the Tail on the Donkey.
Then we will play
Duck for Apples."

"Huh!" said the witch.
"Poor little kids.
What a silly party!
Pin the Tail on the Donkey!"
The old witch flew
back to her cave.
She put the poison ivy
into her brew.
She stirred it
around and around.
Then she tasted it.
"Ho!" she said.
"This brew is just right."
But to make sure,
the old witch put in
two fuzzy caterpillars.

"I have to do something
for those little kids.
They should have more fun.
I know!
I'll have a party for them.
A REAL Halloween party!"
The old witch made a sign.

14

She took the sign to the school.
She put it near the door.
Then she flew back to her cave.

When school was over,
the children ran out.
They saw the sign!

16

"Look!" yelled Jack.

"A big party!

Who wants to go?"

"I'll go," said Jerry.

"We'll go," said Molly and Polly.

"We love a party."

17

The children ran along the path
up the hill.
"Who is giving the party?"
asked Jerry.
"Maybe it's Grandma Petticoat,"
said Molly.
"She gave a Halloween party
for us last year."
"Oh yes," said Jack.
"Grandma was all dressed up
like a ghost.
We played Apple on a String.
We had cider and donuts.
It was lots of fun."
The children ran far,
far up the side of the hill.

"Look!" cried the children.

"There's a cave.

And there's Grandma Petticoat!

She's all dressed up

like a witch!"

"Come in!
Come in, my dearies,"
said the old witch.
"The party is ready.
Come with me."

Jerry tried to look brave.
Molly and Polly laughed,
"Tee-hee-hee!"
They all followed the witch
into her dark old cave.

In the middle of the cave
a fire was burning.
"Sit down," said the witch.
"Sit around the fire, my dearies.
This is my lovely cat.
She will hiss for you."

22

"Stare at the fire, my pet,"
said the witch to her cat.
The black cat stared.
The fire began to dance.
Blue stars flew out
and went "POP!"

"This is Mr. Bones,"
said the old witch.
"He will dance for you."

24

Just then,
three ghosts came in.
They said, "Ooo-oo-oo!"

"Now," said the witch,
"my sweet little spiders
will tickle your ears."
Molly and Polly screamed.
They hugged each other.

"And," said the old witch,

"my rats will run up your arms."

Brave Jerry looked scared.

"Don't worry," said Jack.

"They are only fake ones."

"Here are my
dear little lizards,"
said the witch.
"They will creep
over your shoes."

"Now we will play some games.
First we will play
Toadstool on a String.
Keep your hands
behind your backs."

"Now," said the witch,
"we will play
Duck for Rotten Eggs."

Suddenly,
100 bats flew
all around the cave.

"Are you ready?"
said the witch.
"Now we will play
the best game of all.
Pin the Tail on the Rattlesnake!
A REAL rattlesnake.
Won't that be fun?"

32

"It IS a real rattlesnake!"
yelled the children.
They jumped right out
of their shoes!

The children hopped
like rabbits.
They jumped
over the fire.
They jumped
over the witch.

34

"Let's get out of here,"
yelled Jack.
"She's a real old witch!"
He hopped out of the cave
in three jumps!

"Stop!" called the witch.

"Come back!

I want you to taste

my magic brew.

It will do something funny

to you.

Hee-hee-hee!"

But Jack did not stop.
He hopped all the way
down the hill.
Molly and Polly and Jerry
hopped after him.

The children hopped
down the street,
past Grandma Petticoat's house.
There was Grandma
on the porch!

"See!" cried the children.
"There's Grandma Petticoat!
She's not in the cave.
That was a REAL old witch
for sure!"

The children went on hopping.
At suppertime
they hopped
out of their chairs.
Their mothers took them
to old Doctor Pinkpill.

"Hmm," said Doctor Pinkpill.
"This looks like
the witchy jumps.
I have just the thing for that.
Open your mouths."

The children stopped hopping.

"Come on!" they said.

"Let's go out

for trick or treat."

They rang doorbells.

They yelled, "Trick or treat!"

The children got

lots of candy in their bags.

Old Mr. Crabtree yelled,
"Get away from here,
you kids!"
He didn't give any treats.

So the children tricked him.

"Let's go
to Grandma Petticoat's house,"
the children said.
They rang Grandma's doorbell.
"Trick or treat!" they yelled.

The door flew open.
An old witch
was standing there!
"Hee-hee-hee!"
said Grandma Petticoat.
"Happy Halloween, kids.
Come in to my party."

"The witch! The witch!
Run! Run!"
yelled the children.
"We never want to see
the old witch again."